T0090440

Spirits
of the Mist

The Phantom Publisher

Order this book online at www.trafford.com
or email orders@trafford.com

Most Trafford titles are also available at major online book retailers.

Note for Librarians: A cataloguing record for this book is available from Library and Archives Canada at www.collectionscanada.ca/amicus/index-e.html

Printed in Victoria, BC, Canada.

ISBN: 978-1-4269-1484-3

Library of Congress Control Number: 2009940191

Our mission is to efficiently provide the world's finest, most comprehensive book publishing service, enabling every author to experience success. To find out how to publish your book, your way, and have it available worldwide, visit us online at www.trafford.com

Trafford rev. 10/30/2009

 www.trafford.com

North America & international
toll-free: 1 888 232 4444 (USA & Canada)
phone: 250 383 6864 ✦ fax: 812 355 4082

When a child was born over the ice, the spirit of the child was believed by the Malagwan to enter the child after the child's first warm breath. But if any child was handicapped or malformed at birth that child was suffocated before its first breath to be spared the harsh life of the cold desert of the Arctic. The bodiless spirit of the child was said to wander the ice lands, child minded and vengeful, and the torment of the Eskimo villages across the ice. They were called Jenagoa; mischievous spirits that haunt the ice, always wrecking havoc, and ever ready to play an integral role amongst the living. For, these spirits considered the living fortunate.

ONE

The little Village of Malagwa was like any other Eskimo village in the upper confines of the Arctic because they housed themselves in igloos and lived icy miles away from the next village. Still, there was a significant deviation to the everyday Eskimo Villages. The Malagwan lived in the transient Arctic, dwelling in places somewhere between the transition of Cold Desert Tundra and the thin Conifer Forests. Villages like the Malagwan were spread across this precarious ice land and were always situated close to a strong life force; either a cluster of forest conifers or a permanent water stream. In addition to the deviation, none of these villages were migratory. The villages being non-migratory made villagers like the Malagwan cautious and suspicious of anything and everything, so the Malagwan kept a keen eye on visiting strangers. To the Malagwan, intruders always signified some form of imminent trouble.

The spirits wafted across the lands in a cold Mist. In the very least, they came twice a month, and claimed the lives of whichever child or full grown they could claim. The time these spirits arrived could never be known, near or far apart, but they always arrived under the cover of the rising mist. These spirits entered the Igloos as unhindered as in passing the protecting animal leather that lined the walls of the sleeping family to the lonely hunter exposed in the haunted Woods. There was no hiding from their grip. The death transition was called Sacred Rite of Passage, and it didn't help matters that each family lived quite a distance from one another. Everybody was too concerned with their own fears to bother of the other's sorrows. Still, one family lived the farthest, banished to the outskirts of the little remote village of Malagwa; a single mother and her daughter— Itherica, the demon child.

Only two things brought the village together; trade and festivals. Of these things not even the outlawed could be denied— that mistake would tip the balance of fate, the balance of good and evil, and then the Jenagoa could destroy the village.

"Come quickly, gather around!" Witch Mother called out to the children slugging it out in a fierce game of snowball. The Witch Mother was the Soul Seeker of the Malagwan and conducted Séances for the community. She was fondly called Witch Mother because she told stories by the bonfire on gatherings like these with full fire and light sorcery whenever she felt up for it. The village had gathered under a large tent of wolf fur and dried mat held up by skinned tree stems. Dry thick sticks were spread across the ground as a thick carpet and everyone wore a thick blanket of animal fur. The whole assembly had gathered, no one would stay away or rather be alone, and a big bonfire was being fanned by the Men of the village. The elderly crowded in its warmth and the Malagwan Women made strong wine and herbs for the grown-ups but bittersweet juice for the children. There was merriment and thread music in the tent and every worry dulled under the collective laughter.

"Ah, come over!" Witch Mother said, calling to some children outside the tent. The girls dropped their balls and scurried inside obediently, but the boys laughed and continued pounding each other with snowballs, ignoring Witch Mother with blithe excitement. She returned under the tent to begin the ceremony and soon forgot about the boys.

Spirits of the Mist

"Itherica!" a child yelled across the snow and the boys stopped tossing their snowballs. They were all quiet, frozen in fright. "Stay away from us!" they said frightened, as she approached, her furry footwear sloshing in the snowy ice. She slowly picked up a snowball and juggled it to amuse the boys. They were dead stiff. She tossed the snowball playfully at one of them.

The boys threw away their snowballs and sped at the top of their heels into the tent yelling, "Itherica! Itherica!"

The tent was as quiet as a churchyard by the time Itherica walked in; the cheerfulness seemingly cast out by the demon child. The girl had a small head under her hood and her frail legs made piercing crackles as she walked over the carpet of sticks to the other end of the tent to meet her mother, who was separated from the rest of the company like a waterhole in an ice lake; Malarina was served only water, simple herbs and a morsel of hard cake. Some elderly women hid their faces as the child passed by and Witch Mother waved her hand in exorcism of any unwanted spirits in the tent. After Itherica sat down with her mother, the ceremony slowly returned to life.

Malarina, Itherica's mother, was very thin and pale, impoverished because the village rarely, or at great expense, traded with her. Everyone in Malagwa was in great fear of incurring a curse. Itherica on the other hand was fit and active despite being underfed, and had striking godlike beauty.

The children sang by the bonfire and danced to string music made from tendons. As the music faded the children called for a tale, but no tale was more famous than the happenings of the demon child. It scored a new tale every time.

The Phantom Publisher

"Settle down," Witch Mother gathered the children and signaled for the musical strings to cue to her story. She dipped her hands into her cloak and brought out some dust, sprinkling it over the bonfire; she looked to the demon child and her mother and chanted some incantations. The Soul Seeker began to sing Itherica's tale with a low-key. The fire swayed frighteningly with her every move and gesture and then suddenly lit the whole tent in a heat-deprived blue flame.

TWO

The time of the Nachaga was a form of bitter winter of winter; it was the night season of prolonged darkness across the Arctic, darkness that lasted almost half a year. To prepare for supplies lasting the Nachaga, the Men of the Malagwan hunted under the Wolf Pack for red meat at times accompanied by their sons, while the Women went out to fell trees and gather wood for the community, sometimes accompanied by their daughters. One way or another, the Malagwan made sure there was to be constant trade of supplies from one family to the other, so no one needed to leave the village in the dark season.

6 seasons ago, the Wolf Pack returned to take a head count of all the women and children. Three girls turned up unaccounted for; Etrica, Natrina, and Itherica. But Etrica and Natrina never left the village; the girls had stayed behind playing Seek Me Out among the Igloos.

"Itherica, Itherica! Where was Itherica?" Witch Mother yelled while staring at the girl. Witch mother then groped around the tent, arms stretched, as though she suddenly had been blinded by the cursed child. She continued her tale, "Itherica was lost and late Ithzermus, her father, and head of the Wolf Pack, went frantic leading the Wolf Pack into the Woods to search for his daughter." The old woman's sight seemed to return and Witch Mother looked to Itherica's mother, Malarina, in disdain. Witch Mother continued, "And so the Wolf Pack ignored their families and their very lives to search for Itherica. But that problem was Malarina's, Itherica's mother," Witch Mother pointed to the humble but dejected young woman holding on to Itherica and hiding her face behind the child. "It was her fault, resulting from her negligence; her problem!—their child!" Witch Mother barked like a dog. "Those were dangerous times. Why should all trade their fate for the fate of one?"

Everyone in the tent turned to look at the waterhole of the Malagwan; the irresponsible mother and the cursed child. Itherica always wore a hood to cover her long and dark hair. The child seldom pulled the hood down, but Malarina found ways to shield her conscience from all the attention directed at her. She could spend hours plaiting Itherica's long dark hair, though the child's hair was frail and broke easily at the neckline. She wove it into a half-braid and broke it all up again before the hair was done in simple routine.

The Wolf Pack searched until night time. Fatigued and without any closer to finding Itherica, they revolted under Ithzermus and returned home. Ithzermus went unrelentingly to the late Soul Seeker with a sympathy party. The late Soul Seeker chanted and danced for him and after some hours they finally formed a spiritual séance. The Eye of a Soul Seeker in a séance travels as fast and as broad as the spirit of the earth itself.

"And in the séance the late Soul Seeker could see that child—" Witch Mother pointed a crooked finger at Itherica who was all cuddled up and silent in her mother's lap as her story was being told the nth time in 3 years, all eyes staring piercingly at her, "She saw Itherica purple by the Scaba stream, cold as ice, dead as dust." All the children held their breaths.

Spirits of the Mist

Her mother hid her head in sobs possibly over the memory of her late husband but the Witch Mother continued the story, "But then came along the Mist by the stream to find the corpse of the girl, beautiful and frozen over." Everyone in the tent went on edge over Witch Mother's slightest hint of the Jenagoa spirit.

For some devil-inspired reason the Jenagoa returned the breath of the demon child. Witch Mother's dancing flame lit up the tent in a blaze and so lit up the mixed feelings slouched across everyone's faces, including a small smile across the face of the young Itherica.

"Itherica, Itherica, the spirits called to her like their own, you must trade life for life," Witch Mother aggravated the fire in climaxing her tale, but the man pulling the musical strings nervously lost his key. Although it was funny, no one laughed freely. A young boy stared at Itherica in awe and with fingers beside her temples Itherica made Devil Horns at him. He shrugged away and held tighter to his mother.

"Trade a life for your life, and it must be from no other than your own," Witch Mother continued. Shivers ran down everyone's spines. "And who from our own do you think the Sacred Rite passed on to?" No one dared to answer. Witch Mother took the pleasure of driving home the finale, "The eye of the Seeker spying on her devil works!"

That very instant the Soul Seeker, Ithzermus, and all who participated in the Eye became cold as ice and dead as dust; the warm breath in them hesitant to leave their bodies— Stolen by the Jenagoa over their concern for the selfish demon child.

"You can still feel their warmth in this tent, demanding justice, demanding retribution," Witch Mother waved her hands in supplication. "5 lives for the sake of one. So ever since that time," Witch Mother started citing some incantations and headed for the demon child and her mother, a limp punctuating her walk, "the demon child remains the outcast, the outlaw, and will always be an enemy of the Malagwan."

Nobody minded the tears shed by the girl's mother. A courageous little boy spat in their direction and immediately the boy's mother slapped him hard across the face. Itherica's mother could not take any more pain and humiliation, and stood up with the girl to leave. The whole village parted for her like the Red Sea hoping the worst for the girl and her mother in cryogenic temperatures outside the shelter. Perhaps the Jenagoa would return for the girl and her mother. Young Itherica made faces at everyone as her mother dragged her by the hand across the tent. She scowled at the Witch Mother who didn't hesitate to scowl back, "Jenagoa."

The child was only 8.

THREE

The séances were the commonest of the spiritual acts of the Malagwan. The Eye told of the past with the spirit of the earth witnessing everything since the world began. The eye told of the present with the spirit of the wind blowing across the earth. The eye told of the future, by the spirit of fire and water, the mystery elements not limited by time. The men of the Wolf Pack had gathered for a séance and the Soul Seeker was in preparations to summon the Eye. The men were poised for the uneventful, but a hard-faced man, Illikus, head of the Wolf Pack, was braced for anything.

The Soul Seeker danced around the fire as the men kept silent, watching her every move and humming to her melody. "Oh spirit of the earth, wind, fire and water, heed our call." It was typical for her to be about the place, hopping and singing until something extraordinary happens. The men were waiting for that moment. The moment she would supernaturally start to hover in midair but quiet as a mouse. At that moment they would drift her over the bonfire so she wouldn't freeze over, and wait for her to babble; babble about something or anything familiar.

The moment had arrived and the Witch Mother began to wail. "Ohh," she moaned. "Ohh no. I see destruction. I see war. I see Death."

The Phantom Publisher

The men of the Wolf Pack were confused. "War? Death?" Who was stupid enough to engage war in such terrible times?

"I see pain," witch mother moaned, "so much pain."

"Is it in the future? Was it the past?" the men spoke to her, though they understood she could not hear a thing or speak back.

Witch Mother shook while suspended in thin air. "I see Itherica. Itherica!!" she said in anguish and then she started to cry uncontrollably.

"I knew surely we had not seen the last of that child!" one of the men snapped, and looked to the others already gathered in a circle around the hovering Soul Seeker. She slowly started to exhale cold air.

"This is strange, but what has the Demon Child got to do with war?" some of the men of the Wolf Pack started to ask themselves but looking to their leader, Illikus, for counsel.

"I've never seen her like this before; I've had enough. Wake her up!" Illikus commanded but the moment the men reached out to pull the Soul Seeker to the ground she started raving like a lunatic. "I see Jenagoa! Jenagoa!!"

The men fell behind, totally taken aback. A strange gust blew into the tent and the bonfire went out as easily as a matchstick. It was pitch dark and everyone noticed the sudden chill in the tent.

"And I see them. They will bring war for their own. They come for Itherica," the Soul Seeker whispered from somewhere across the floor in midst of the darkness. Some men ran out of the tent while the few that remained lit their torches to help Witch Mother to her feet. Her hands were as cold as ice and they discovered her body was robbed of breath before their eyes.

The Malagwan had had it with the demon child. They were all frightened by the death of the Soul Seeker and what's more of the visions she had not the privilege of clarifying. Everyone had gathered and the assembly had drawn a conclusion; Itherica only meant more trouble.

"We have lost two seekers to this child, the girl and her mother must be sent away," Illikus recited to the gathered counsel," for it appears we are bound to lose more."

"But what about the balance of fate?" some of the villagers replied apprehensively. "Will we not encounter more evil?"

"We reiterated the words of the Soul Seeker," Illikus retorted, "I fear that balance has already been tipped. The Jenagoa scheme as we speak. More will die."

"Illikus," a seated wise old man called to him. His name was Izuk. He was head of the village counsel. These wise men had been seated before anyone else. "If we have not heard those precise words from the Soul Seeker we must not believe all is lost." The counsel looked to the demon child and her mother already assembled with them. Izuk continued, "But how do we get rid of this pestilence among us without causing more chaos?"

Illikus spoke out loud, "All what I know is what the Soul Seeker said, the Jenagoa will come for this child. And will visit evil on us. Set this child free to them, so they need not come."

The populace cheered and clapped in support. The elders mused then looked to the girl's mother, "Malarina, will you be willing to let the child roam free?"

The girl's mother was full of tears. "If she leaves, she'll die. Don't let her die. She doesn't know a thing."

Izuk felt pity for the young mother's dilemma, "Then you can't abandon her, and we fear we have no other choice but to banish you alongside her. Ready your belongings, after the passing of the next blizzard you will head for Balawaq Village, perhaps its citizens will be kind enough to let you stay."

All gathered were cheering and roaring on the decision taken by the elders of the Malagwan, but Malarina and the Demon Child left downcast.

FOUR

The true nature of a blizzard is only known by those who know it to be common weather. To the small colony of research scientists in one of the most extreme habitats in the World, it was a remarkable weather to watch from within the shelter of their warm, cozy facility and labs. Unfortunately, it was also deadly weather. A blizzard in the Arctic consisted of cryogenic snowballs and snowflakes tiny enough to freeze your lungs over if you do not protect your whole face. A blizzard at times consisted of hail stones, the sizes of which the Malagwan believed to measure the temperament of the spirits. These hailstones were capable of inflicting injury; injury ranging from the meanest possible headache to a murderous blow, a blow comparable to that from a baseball bat. But the most frightening of all, was the least spoken of all— a blizzard could toy with the senses. Without a proper map or some sort of compass not even the Eskimos could find their way.

Captain Cain Cook and his pals played foosball in the living quarters for the NASA boys, and he was their pilot. They had received radio from a station 12 miles out that the weather was going to be remarkable, and since the weather pretty much always had a way to screw with the indoor research as it did to everything outside the facility, the group of 7 scientists just wanted to lounge the afternoon away in the NASA facility. Cain Cook was a proud father and he didn't mind bringing Ben along with him for the 3-week expedition into the Arctic. Cain Cook stood with his colleagues over a game of foosball, but Ben was up and about the facility looking for anything to keep his mind occupied on this weather-christened Sabbath day.

"Picky tulip," Capt. Cook smirked while chewing his cigar as he rattled the box of foosball, "but you can call me old fashioned!" He slapped a goal in and raised his hands cheerfully in the air. He had won. Cain could boast he was an inch taller than anyone else in the group, so having his long hands in the air made everyone else pretend to be upset.

Some of his colleagues jumped on him, noisily, carousing in delight and laughing wildly. There was a woman among them, Elizabeth Hoodwinks; she had two jobs. She was a lab scientist but also a special assistant to Dr. Crawford. Yet Elizabeth was a tomboy, so the scientists still referred to themselves by the nickname, the NASA boys.

Ben Cook was done playing inside the shelter hours ago. The little boy had gone outside to ski. Although cautioned by the grown-ups to remain within sighting distance, Ben was soon out of sight. It didn't take long for Diego, a dark haired and beardy rock scientist, to notice the little boy was gone since Diego had only just arrived from a voyage into the Iceland.

"Cook? Where's your boy?" he asked as he roughed up his beards with the palms of his hands to warm up his frozen cheeks.

Cain Cook was as stiff as a conifer. Compared with Diego, Cain had no beards so it was easy noticing his face turning white, as white as snow.

Everyone took to the search around the small facility.

"Ben? Ben!" They yelled as they patrolled the grounds.

Ben Cook was nowhere to be found and it had already begun to snow. Everybody knew in time the snow would fade off Ben's tracks, so time was of the essence.

They found tracks to a tethered dog sledge. It was Diego's sledge. He had come in with it only minutes ago. Now it was gone. Ben had taken it.

The NASA facility was located at the edge of a hill and the boy's sledge tracks led to the edge of that hill. Cain Cook was furious with himself.

The other side of the hill tailed in a gentle slope, but it was a gentle slope that tapered downhill well nigh 2 miles with trees astraddle. And things were turning out for the worse; the snow was burying the sledge tracks sooner than they could search out any meaningful portion of the slope.

"Ben!" Captain Cook and the NASA boys yelled at the top of their voices downhill. The echo of their voices yelled back at them and over the snow-covered trees. There was no sign of Ben in the building snow blanket all around them and the falling snow began to harden into balls.

"Cook, we will find Ben," they tried to console him, "But—"

"I will not abandon him," the Captain snapped. "Ben!" he screamed aloud even deeper.

"Not in this weather," the NASA boys tried to pacify him, but contemplated secretly if it was necessary to use force.

"Cain, we aren't going to abandon him!" Nathaniel was Cain Cook's best friend since high school, witty, reasonable with a fair share of ambition. He was a Mathematician and Field Scientist, so to the NASA boys he was jovially counted as 2 men and dubbed so. "Ben is a smart kid; he'd be looking out for himself maybe up in a cozy tree to wait out this blizzard. Be smart yourself. Don't get yourself killed."

"He is only 6 years old Nathan!" Capt. Cook retorted, and yelled again into the rising winds, "Ben!"

The NASA boys began to drag him back into the facility and did it with a great bit of difficulty. When he was in, he looked into their eyes and sobbed. "I have failed him Nathaniel. I failed my boy."

There were 7 electronic sledges in the facility and 4 dog sledges. By the time, the blizzard numbed in the slightest they were planning on combing the slope. A little fear insidiously polluted the hope that all was not lost, for a full blown blizzard could go on for 3 days unabated.

A Dogsled was excellent for moving across the ice. It could have up to 4 or more dogs strapped evenly with leather belts, and having a huge head dog leading the pack. The NASA boys also found other ways to use the dogsleds for fun. It was excellent for racing. Cain, Uncle Nathan, Diego and all the NASA boys found time racing the dogsleds down slope and back up during leisure hours. Unfortunately, it was much too wild for Ben. He had to stay indoors playing board games or by the door side making snowballs. But today he had an overdose. Diego and others had just returned from an expedition out in the ice. Ben had found Uncle Diego's dogsled still strapped and warm by the edge of the slope and just wanted to take it for a 5 minutes ride down slope. Unfortunately, the moment he tugged the steering straps of the dogsled Ben didn't know how to stop the speeding dogs, but held on for dear life. The facility on the top of the hill disappeared in seconds and all that was left was for him to enjoy the ride to nowhere.

Spirits of the Mist

It was now 3 hours and the dogs had grown weary, so it was the first time he could safely step out of the sledge. He was cold, tired, frightened and hungry. It seemed like the cold was getting at him despite all the thick clothes and boots he was wearing. But worse still, a thick fog had begun to rise. Ben was deep in trouble.

FIVE

"Why don't you feel like playing today?" a voice from the mist asked disgruntled.

Itherica was surrounded by mist, and she warmed her hands by rubbing them together.

"I don't feel like it," Itherica snapped angrily.

"You don't like playing with us anymore, Itherica," another voice replied; a shrill voice in the mist that seemed to appear as a girl and disappear as quickly.

"No, but why do I have to be the one always seeking?" Itherica pursed her lips, "I only got tired."

Five ghostly shapes of children stepped out from the misty cloud surrounding Itherica for their usual game of Seek Me Out.

"Well then, you can have it your way, but only for today," one of the spirits replied, the spirit that sounded like a girl. "Pick whom among us will be It."

Itherica smiled and tried to touch one of them; the one that looked like a boy. He suddenly appeared behind her. "This is going to be too easy," he chuckled trying to scare her.

"Wait!" one of the spirits suddenly said aloud and all the spirits seemed to look in the same direction. "There is a little boy all alone. I can taste his fear. He's been sweating," the spirit chuckled, "And, his dogs are worn out."

Itherica looked to the direction they were watching, "Is he nearby?" she asked, concerned.

"Very near," they said, "you could see him, if the mist wasn't so thick."

"You guys better don't do anything!" Itherica yelled without realizing she was yelling, and slowly walked in that direction. The Jenagoa faded into the mist then the mist gently began to lift.

It was only funny trying to see the boy feed some left over biscuits to the dogs. The boy had loosened one of the leather belts that restrained the dogs to the sled and was trying to loosen the other when Itherica came by, but the boy didn't realize he was dropping some of his biscuits on the snowy ground. He looked clumsy.

"Qu nad a mas?" Itherica had asked from behind him. She meant *What are you doing?*

Ben was shocked to see someone appear from nowhere. Fortunately, the mist was beginning to thin out. She looked like a girl under that hood but much smaller and probably much younger than he was. "Qu nad a mas!" she had repeated softly and the native girl pulled down her hood. Her hair and eyes were black, black as night, and she had a healthy color to her skin. She approached him.

Ben didn't want to squeal and she didn't look like she was going to harm him, but he was lost and didn't know what to expect, so he took a pair of cautious steps away from her. Adamantly, she walked up to him and strangely took the leather belt from him. He breathed deeply and backed away from the dogsled a little frightened at her stern approach. She re-tied the leather strongly to the frame of the sledge, and shook her head at him. "Ni can qu nad a mas?" which meant, 'You obviously don't know what you are doing?'

She stretched her hands to him and pulled a glove from his hands. She threw the hand glove at one of the dogs and the dog charged at it and bit it hungrily, but the dog was well restrained by the leather belts and sledge.

Ben was dumbfounded. Then he smiled sheepishly, "I see, hungry dogs."

The mist had cleared completely and only one igloo was in sight. Itherica reached for the steering straps and led the dogsled to her home. Ben followed from behind, a lot frightened, a lot confused, yet a lot delighted.

The blizzard had only shown signs of relenting when Cain Cook left on his sledge, headed in no particular direction but downhill. The NASA boys never knew he was gone, until he was gone. Someone had raided the arsenal behind the lab. The person took a shotgun, a rifle, and enough ammunition to kill off a pack of wolves. That person's sled trail led downhill.

Captain Cain Cook, Ben's dad, had been a volunteer for Save the Wildlife and Forest foundation, but the pilot had never gone hunting in his life—that made things worse for him. Although the air captain was fortified as an armadillo with ammunition, the NASA boys truly doubted he'd be able to fire a single bullet, needless to say, aim properly. It was foolish for Cain to go out alone, so the NASA boys grouped the rest of the ammo and readied their sledges to head downhill after the trail before it went cold. The blizzard had only lightened to snowing.

"Cain! Ben!" Nathan yelled as the group of 6 raced downhill. On the other hand, Nathan was skilled in hunting. The other NASA boys, even Elizabeth the lab scientist, could handle their weapons fine if the need ever came, so no one in the team stayed behind to watch the facility. Everyone was concerned for both father and son. The weather in the cold lands was very sly and could be downright mean, so everyone knew the lightening blizzard could take a bad turn for worse; neither were the fierce animals that lived in the cold forests ever imagined to be friendly. It now depended on whom or what would get to whom first.

"Captain Cain! Ben O' boy! Hello!" the NASA boys yelled as they raced their sleds downhill, with the winds growing stronger by the minute.

SIX

Many people have their own ideas of what an Igloo should look like. The traditional igloos looked like a tea cup turned on its top with a long corridor leading into it. But an igloo could be rectangular, circular or whatever shape it was made as. Only one thing made an Igloo an Igloo. The outsides were made of hard and tough blocks, but the insides were made of soft comfortable animal hide, which made the Igloo oddly warm, sometimes, as warm as tropical weather.

Ben Cook was lost. The native girl had kept his sled safe in what functions same as a modern garage. The girl's mother never appeared startled by the boy's appearance. Both girl child and mother had strangely stared at him all day till night, but finally they had gone to bed. Ben took time before he ate what they had given him to eat. It also took a while before he dared to fall asleep. They all slept in the cramped Igloo. Many hours after, it slowly began to get colder. Mist began seeping into the Igloo through the animal fur, and it didn't take long before a ghostly hand fingered around Itherica's foot.

She raised her head and felt the wetness in the air. Itherica lit an oil lamp beside her and the yellow light lit up as blurry in the mist, hardly giving much light to the little Igloo. "What now?" Itherica answered, trying to hide her reluctance.

"You didn't return to play," the voice answered a little peeved. It sounded like a boy Jenagoa.

"I was occupied," she replied reluctantly.

The apparition soared about the little igloo flying over everybody. It danced around the little boy and Itherica grew apprehensive.

"Hmm? Who's your new friend?" The Jenagoa's face appeared above the fatigued Ben Cook. Ben had been sleeping soundly but soon enough his face slowly began to pale under the cold watch of the floating spirit. The warm breaths he took in soon started to expire in cold thick wisps.

"Ok. We'll play tomorrow," retorted Itherica. "Just go. You're making it too cold in here for everybody."

The spirit disappeared and reappeared behind her. "O touchy, are you? It seems like you like him, don't you?" The Jenagoa reformed his face into the face of Ben and smiled devilishly.

"Shut up, don't say that!" Itherica retorted irked, but with a blush.

The Jenagoa chuckled and floated to the ceiling of the igloo. "We'll be outside at Illikus' house. We are cooking him a surprise. But you will join us tomorrow in the woods, Itherica." He seemed to fade away from the roofing and immediately everywhere began to warm up. But before he left he added, "By the way, don't forget to bring your new friend."

The room gradually became as warm as before and Ben all wrapped up in himself coughed gently. Itherica frowned then grimaced as she looked at Ben, and then covered him up in a sheet of sewed animal fur. Ben crouched tightly under the spread without realizing it.

At that moment there was loud banging on the igloo door. A very loud bang and Itherica shook in her fears for the worst.

A Map contains anything important in a place. Most of the Ice lands were unchartered or chartered wrongly but Cain Cook hoped the Eskimo Village of Malagwa would be where the map said it would be. He breathed a deep "thank goodness" when he found a smoke signal from a part of the settlement up a huge cliff. He was only a few hours ride to the village but nighttime had come and he needed to seek shelter among the trees above the grounds. He tethered his sled and fed his dogs with meat, but Cain Cook constantly worried about Ben. Both father and son were a splitting image of one another body and soul and that made Cain Cook worry all the more. He had blonde hair but not very healthy blue eyes, so had to wear reading glasses as a child. His son, Ben, also wore reading glasses, so Cain Cook worried on how clumsy and naïve he could be when he was 6. Nighttime had come, but he couldn't sleep a wink.

Nathan and the NASA boys were battling it out through the blizzard. The blizzard had taken to a strong gust hurling cold but small ice balls behind them. Luckily for the NASA boys the blizzard wasn't blowing against them, so they could continue unhindered through the night. The captain had taken Diego's most necessary map, now all they were left to work with Diego's other hard to use maps and their compasses. It made it harder to catch up, but they knew the Cooks would be headed for someplace warm and homely. Malagwa was the closest settlement in that direction and Cain Cook's trail was already warming up.

SEVEN

The big bang woke Ben up. The fright across Itherica's face was clear for him to see. Itherica's mother went to answer the door.

"No," Itherica beckoned, "Jenagoa out there."

Malarina caressed Itherica's cheek to calm her down then went to open the door. A big strong person was waiting. It was Illikus.

"I'm sorry we cannot leave this night, if we leave we will die or lose our way, the blizzard is still strong." Itherica's mother said humbly.

"I'm not here for that," he barged into the Igloo letting in a waft from the cold blizzard outside. Illikus headed straight for the 8 year old demon child. "The Jenagoa want Izuk. He is dying," he said to Malarina without looking at her and stumping snow off his feet, "I have come here to make you know, I'll not let the demon child take him."

He glowered down at Itherica and scowled at her. Itherica was frightened by his huge physic and scurried behind Ben, but even Ben was trembling. Illikus was as shocked to see Ben as Ben was as shocked to see Illikus.

"A boy?" Illikus hesitated as he stared down at the boy. His face was hysterical. "You've been hiding a stranger among us? You heap curses on us," he stated to Malarina.

"No please," Malarina beckoned and held Illikus by the hand. "Itherica found him stray out in the open ice. We were going to present him to Izuk by morning then leave."

Illikus mused for a while and then crouched on his knees. "He must see Izuk. Where did you find the boy?" Illikus asked Malarina.

Malarina was nervous. "Itherica found him and his dogsled close to the Valley Inlet."

Illikus took off the animal fur blanket from Ben to examine if he was wounded. "He looks well. He must be a son of a foreign stranger. By any chance do you know what he calls himself?"

"Ben. My name is Ben," the boy answered to the surprise of everybody, including Itherica.

Illikus jumped to his feet. "You understand our language?" he asked in astonishment. Ben hadn't realized he was speaking Malagwan. He was beginning to tremble. What was going on? He nodded slowly to Illikus.

Illikus stretched out his hand to Ben. "You must come with me, young Ben. You're not safe here with the demon child."

As Ben stretched out his hand to receive the hand of Illikus, the fright in Itherica suddenly transformed into rage. Astonishingly, she pounced on Illikus like a cat. "No. I found him! Why won't you mind your own business!" she yelled shouting and scratching on Illikus. Malarina grabbed Itherica in the panic of what Illikus might do to her, "Itherica!"

Illikus almost forgot who Itherica was and was nigh hitting her in defense. He scrambled away from her as her mother restrained her. "He's my friend and you don't touch him!" Itherica scowled at the head of the Wolf Pack. Illikus felt a little blood ooze from the fingernail scratches she had inflicted on his face and looked at Ben. Itherica grinned then made a chuckle, taunting Illikus, "Jenagoa are not here for Izuk. No, Izuk is going to live. They are at your house. It is your blood they want. So go mind your business!"

"No that's a lie," Illikus retorted, escaping from the Igloo. He had left his home unwatched out of concern for Izuk. It was known by the Malagwan as *styoud nustaje*; the commonplace mistake.

A Natural disaster on the cliffs and mountain ranges in the cold Arctic North was an avalanche, and it had a subtle way of taking the valleys and hillsides by surprise. An avalanche was a sudden sweep of either snow, or more dangerously, chunks of ice or on some occasions both; mixed like milk and oats down steep slopes. In full swing, it was usually preceded by a low rumbling sound and a quiet earth tremor. No one knows the true causes of an avalanche but the Malagwan believe its origins were not of this world and that avalanches were controlled by spirit forces, and that reason alone made it special; disquietingly special to mountaineers, lone rangers and cliff hangers, but amusingly special to the Jenagoa. Unfortunately if the Malagwan had told the NASA boys that story, the NASA boys would have laughed it off, and laughed hard. But an amusing coincidence was that the Jenagoa spirits would have laughed right along with them.

No one heard the quiet rumble that night. The NASA boys had met Cain Cook screaming at the top of his lungs in agony, and it was obvious what was making him scream out of control. "No! Ben! No not Ben!"

An avalanche had spilled across the mountain pass that led to the Eskimo Village. It had buried the pass under meters and meters of snow and ice.

"Cain, come get out of the snow, more could cave!" Nathan said to his best friend, as he and Diego tried pulling the captain out of the freezing ice. The captain had been trying to dig his way through the huge mass of snow that now blocked the inlet to Malagwa, but it was hopeless. Anytime he swiped out a little snow and ice, more snow and ice fell into its place.

"Come on, it'll take you years to dig through this and that's if it doesn't re-crystallize and harden like a rock mass," Diego added to dissuade the captain.

"Leave me alone, Nathan." Captain Cook struggled as the NASA boys tried to restrain him, his exposure to severe cold could result in hypothermia. "My boy's just through there."

"You must look at yourself, captain," Diego replied, both men finally succeeded in pinning the aircraft pilot to the ground. "You are exhausted. It's too cold and you haven't eaten. We barely have any strength left to get back to the facility."

"This is madness. What use are you to Ben if you end up sick or dead?" Nathan said, calming the pilot down. Cain Cook slowly let himself breathe normally and calmly, but his eyes were covered in tears and his nose brought out fluid. "I almost found him Nathan, my friend. His trail leads through that pass. He's with a dogsled," The captain said trying to hold back his tears like a man. "This trail must have disappeared completely by now."

"Your boy should be alright," Diego replied comparing his maps to the one he got off the captain, "that Pass leads to the Eskimo Village of Malagwa. You can't miss it if you take it."

"That's logical," Nathan said. "Those dogs are native bred. They know this area. I am sure the dogs must have headed for the nearest choice of safety at the faintest feel of fatigue. Don't worry Cain, the Malagwan people might be unwelcoming but they aren't savages. I've met some on one of our expeditions," Nathan assured, "We'll find your boy. We just have to find another way into the Eskimo Village."

Diego took a deep study of the map from the captain's dogsled and shook his head in disappointment. "The only way across that pass is around this mountain to the other side. It will take days to get there. We need to get back to the facility. I think we all need all the rest we can get for that journey."

'Captain Cook. Come on get up. You'll freeze to death in this snow." All the NASA boys came to help the air captain to his feet.

"At least we know the boy will be safe," Nathan said patting the aircraft pilot on the shoulder. They got on their dogsleds and started home bound.

EIGHT

The travelling avalanche might have not been able to hurt any of the NASA boys but it did hurt someone. It had swallowed up whole the home of Illikus and by morning the Eskimo Village of Malagwa was in mourning.

Malarina went outside the Igloo to ready the dogs for the journey to the next village. The blizzard had finally stopped and left a heavy carpet of snow covering the ground. But, something strange had happened because everyone in Malagwa was up early. A crowd of onlookers had surrounded Malarina's home, and just stared blankly at Malarina, but they were careful to stand a good distance from the Igloo.

"Mother?" Itherica got off sleeping outside her sleeping blanket. "Mother?" she called again and looked to Ben who was still asleep. She grimaced then kicked him gently at the knee. Ben was already beginning to wake up when Itherica saw the door to the Igloo still opened. "Mother shut the door. Has the blizzard stopped?"

Itherica walked out of the Igloo and found her mother quiet as a winter mouse with the snow cover almost to her knees. "What's the matter?" she asked, not lifting her head to see the village community standing around their home, watching them. "What's the matter?" she asked again wading through the snow to shake one of Malarina's arms. Her mother shook in fright when Itherica touched her, at first not realizing it was Itherica. At that moment Itherica saw the entire village gathered around her house.

Izuk and Illikus were the only ones that approached from the distance. Their steps were timed and Illikus appeared to be carrying a boy child in his hands. The boy was still sleeping Itherica thought, but when Illikus got to the demon child and her mother he dropped to his knees, painfully burying his thighs in the snow. He showed the boy to the demon child and Itherica sloshed behind her mother in fright when she saw his pale skin color.

"He was about to join the Wolf Pack," Illikus cried and sobbed quietly. "Next week he would have been 12."

The boy was pale, very pale. He was as pale as white ash.

"Mommy, please?" Itherica begged burying her face deep into her mother's back. "Make Illikus go away?"

Izuk, the old man, on the other hand was looking healthier than ever. He tried to support Illikus, the Head of the Wolf Pack, on his frail old body. He looked to Malarina, Itherica's mother; she was near tears in sympathy then yelled very loudly for all to hear, all of whom included any spirits lurking nearby. "We have come to seek your forgiveness on behalf of Illikus and how much trouble he has caused you and the demon child—" he said, twisting his face in hatred and disconcertment, "—and for our evil intentions in trying to send you away!"

Malarina tried to console sobbing Illikus but they shied away very quickly.

Izuk continued his speech. "You can continue to stay with us to preserve the balance and I swear that anyone who bothers you or refuses to trade with you is banished from our lands. You can live and move freely as you have always done long before."

Itherica's face brightened immediately she heard those words. "Thank you so much," she said gently, putting out her face. She was totally delighted to hear that she could move freely and play without restraint, but Malarina cautiously protected her from going to meet both men. The people of the village weren't accepting their lonely family from the heart. They were accepting them because they had to. Itherica's mother bowed in gratitude and Itherica bowed very quickly but then raised her head with a glad smile.

When Izuk saw the demon child smile he took Illikus away to try to restore the boy. The whole village followed them. Ben was watching from the door and his fear of the strange girl child, Itherica, grew with every moment. Itherica hopped about, she couldn't have been more delighted.

Watching Itherica all the time was the only way Ben could feel safe, but Itherica didn't care if he followed her about. Ben was following quite a safe distance behind. He never wanted her out of his sight.

"Don't follow me!" she said every once in a while, but he still did. It was odd they couldn't understand each other by morning since only a night ago Ben could hear and speak Malagwan.

That morning wasn't turning out for Itherica the way she thought it would. They had walked through the village and no one was welcoming. All they had received were shut doors and emptied streets. Anyway, the Eskimo village had good excuse, it was the day after a blizzard and the snow was heavy. Itherica was so naïve, but then she met some naughty boys playing afar off on a field on her way back to the Igloo. They were playing snowballs with the snowmen they had made. She was delighted and skipped towards them but by the time she had bent to gather snow to make a snowball they muttered, "Jenagoa" then scrambled away to go play somewhere safe. When Itherica got home, she made herself a snowman and danced around it, pretending to play with herself and trying not to cry.

She saw Ben watching her cry. "Go away," she said sulky, pushing Ben into the little igloo, though she knew Ben didn't understand a word she was saying. "Stay away."

She didn't need Ben's company, but after a while Ben could hear her sobbing by the Igloo. He found Itherica squatting in the thick snow, alone with her snowman, which wasn't looking like it was having a nice time either.

"Don't be a crybaby," Ben said to her, "You don't have to cry. I'll play with you." When he touched her shoulder, he saw a lot of tears in her eyes, but also a lot of confusion. She didn't understand him and shoved his hand off her winter coat. "Leave me alone!" Itherica snapped.

Ben felt sorry for her and how she was feeling. She had no friends. He made a snowball and knocked the head off her snowman. Itherica didn't care and sat in her sulk. He made another snowball and threw it at her. After he threw it the second time she looked up to him and yelled some words in Malagwan. Ben gave up trying to comfort her and sat away on his own, hoping for his father to arrive anytime soon. Little Ben had his own worries to worry about.

After he sat for a while, someone threw a snowball at him. The cold snowball broke into his warmer and he jumped up. He saw Itherica holding three snowballs and a wry smile. He smiled back and dug his fingers through a large chunk of snow. The game was on

NINE

Anyone can catch a smile as easily as everyone can catch a cold, but much different from an unhealthy sneeze was the magic a healthy smile worked in dispelling uncomfortable feelings like fear and insecurity. Itherica and Ben realized it when they raced the dogsled. Ben had sneezed over Itherica's winter coat as they both grappled the dog leash hanging on for dear life, and as they raced the pack of dogs across the white snow, it had been the first time Ben saw her smile. She had a brilliant set of teeth. Ben never saw that before. And again he never saw that she was a wild racer. For the first time since he'd been lost, he was smiling on seeing her smile. And they had both forgotten how lonely they were. The dogsled had stopped and Itherica saw him stare at her, enamored. She smiled sheepishly and pulled off the hood from her winter coat so he could have a good look. That made Ben blush and he looked away. She was pretty, but he didn't care.

She said something in Malagwan and slapped his head playfully, but so hard he tripped over his loosened bootlaces.

"Ouch, you hit like my dad," he said, smarting over her boyish behavior, but he knew she never understood whatever he said.

She jumped off the sled and spun herself in circles until she went dizzy and fell in the snow.

"Things must be going really well for you now," Ben said dusting off snow from his clothes and tying up his bootlaces. After a while, Ben asked without a second thought, "So why do they call you Jenagoa then run off?"

Itherica suddenly stiffened like she'd heard a ghoulish shriek. She hadn't understood him but it was clear she had heard the word Jenagoa. Her cheeks began to redden.

"No, don't go angry," Ben slowly rose to his feet to apologize. "Oh, no, I didn't call you Jenagoa."

She said some words in Malagwan and ran for home leaving Ben alone with the dogsled. He saw her run off towards the Igloo and his shoulders slumped in disappointment. He had hurt her feelings, maybe. But when he rounded the dogs and pulled the dogsled toward the little Igloo he saw Itherica running past the Igloo into the woods. That was strange. When he got to the Igloo he left the dogsled and saw Malarina by the door. "Stop her, she might get lost or hurt?" he said to her mother, pointing to Itherica scuttling through the woods behind the Igloo, but Malarina only shriveled behind the door to the igloo. The woods frightened him but reluctantly he followed Itherica into the eerie woods. Malarina peeped out of the Igloo to watch Ben follow her daughter's trail. She whispered a prayer in Malagwan as the brave boy ventured into the woods, not knowing what he might encounter, and she feared he was bound to meet Itherica's other friends.

Many minutes into the woods, running in no particular direction he could make note of, someone pushed Ben to the ground from within the trees. "Why are you following me, boy?" Itherica had said and it sounded like she wasn't speaking Malagwan but plain English because Ben could understand her. Or maybe she was speaking Malagwan and he could understand Malagwan.

"Do you always jump on people like that?" Ben replied rising to his feet, checking his arm for anything broken.

"So you hear me now? I wonder how come, a minute ago you clearly couldn't hear or speak a thing," Itherica mused scratching through her dark hair. She saw him checking his arm and slapped him across the arm. "No silly, nothing's happened to your arm. If something was wrong you'd already be in tears. I thought I told you to wait. Why did you follow me here, it's not safe."

"You didn't tell me anything," Ben replied and dusted snow off his body.

"Oh right, you couldn't understand me, well now you can so go back," she replied pointing into the woods behind Ben. Ben hesitated. Everywhere in the forest looked the same. A step away from Itherica and Ben would be lost.

"Not safe from what?" Ben ignored her pestering and looked around the empty snowy woods.

"Oh I'm late!" she exclaimed immediately but before they could say anything else a gentle mist began to cloud the woods. "They are here," Itherica said gently and held Ben's hand. "Shhh," she whispered putting a finger to her lips, "Follow me. Don't talk until I tell you to."

"Why?" Ben whispered back. "Jenagoa?"

"Don't say that, they don't like to be called that," Itherica replied. They walked deeper into the Mist and the mist thickened even more, and then Itherica said, "They are my friends and I am late."

The Phantom Publisher

"You can count on that!" a voice replied from nowhere and breathtakingly the mist cleared. It just disappeared into nothing. "I see you brought along the pipsqueak?" the voice jeered.

TEN

A Cleared area in the woods suddenly appeared from nowhere and there was no one else there but Ben and Itherica, or that was what Ben thought.

"Everybody, this is Ben," Itherica announced to no particular person, "Ben say hello to my friends." Ben couldn't resist staring around the area and peering through the trees. Maybe Itherica was seeing things; there was no one else in the woods. Itherica nervously pinched Ben's hand with her long fingernails.

"Ouch, Hello," Ben said out to no particular person and took his hand from Itherica.

"I can see why you like him," a girl voice spoke from very close by, frighteningly close by. "He's such a klutz."

Ben turned around in reflex, his heartbeat rising.

"Why is he staring? I don't like him staring," another voice said, a little peeved. It was a boy voice.

"Stop turning around," Itherica whispered to Ben from a side of her mouth and he froze.

Ben's eyes were beginning to dart around like sardines.

"He's not staring," Itherica replied in defense, "How can he stare if you don't let him see you?"

"Is that so? Now she's going to bring all her village snowballing pipsqueaks here to see us," the boy voice said ironically, and both Itherica and Ben felt a very cold and unpleasant gust brush past them.

"No," Itherica retorted, "He is with me because he's my friend. Just like you guys."

After she said that there was an unnerving silence.

"He's the boy in the snow," the girl voice stated. "I remember him. But why did you bring him here?" the girl voice asked. A question Itherica knew she couldn't answer.

"It's because I told her to," a different boy voice answered, it sounded older and a bit more menacing. "I wanted someone new to play with." The deep boy voice sounded right around Itherica and soon enough a face appeared in a puff beside her left side. It disappeared just as quickly as it appeared.

Ben pointed in bewilderment and Itherica quickly held down his arm. "Don't point."

"You all should show yourselves to our new friend and not leave him confused," the menacing voice commanded and Ben felt he was about to experience something he'd rather not.

A light cloud like a ball fell down from somewhere among the trees and rolled out three figures. They appeared as two boys and a girl, all of the same height. The unusual thing was they were made wholly of misty vapor, and at times if you looked just right, you could see right through them. It was a wow sight.

"You see them?" Itherica asked grinning from ear to ear on seeing the startled look on Ben's face.

Ben nodded very cautiously.

Itherica proceeded to introduce them. "That is Luc, Tica, and Dale," she pointed, "Dale doesn't talk, so don't talk to him," Itherica added in a light cheer but Ben didn't have the nerve to smile.

"And I am Kyle," the deepest of boy voices spoke again and appeared right in front of Ben. He had a big smile on his face, a smile that showed no teeth. Ben lost his footing and fell in the snow but Itherica helped him up in a laugh.

"So what games are we playing with these warm bloods today?" Tica asked impatiently, and Luc hissed at her excitement to play with the new boy.

"Yes, what game are we playing Kyle?" Itherica asked, eager to get things rolling. Everyone looked to Kyle to tell them what to do. He was the smartest by some fifty years.

"Well, I have cooked up a special game since we are having a special friend to play," Kyle replied, no one could tell if there was delight in his tone or menace. "It's a game of tag team-tag team. Let's pair up; Luc will pair Tica and—" Kyle was just about to pair himself with Itherica when Itherica spoke up.

"Good," Itherica replied totally thrilled, "Ben and I will pair up. Kyle can referee."

"Fine," Kyle said exasperatedly, but in his voice was a subtle tone of jealousy, "have it your way Itherica." He disappeared for a moment.

"This is going to be fun," Itherica said to Ben squeezing his arm warmly. She hadn't noticed she had been holding

Ben's hand all the time. But the Jenagoa spirits noticed. And Kyle noticed.

"Up here!" Kyle re-appeared floating high between the tree tops. Itherica and Ben had to cock their heads to see him. "The first team to find the twin twig of the twig I hold in my hand wins. It's lying somewhere on open ground. Begin."

The Eskimo village had just begun the ceremony. It was an initiation ceremony to select the new Soul Seeker. Illikus and the Wolf Pack had gathered for the séance. The community of Malagwa waited outside the meeting tent to know who the new Soul Seeker was. The spirits of the elements only chose a woman and were very choosy. It usually took hours but today it took no time at all. There must have been something somebody had to witness for the elements seemed to be waiting for the séance. The first woman to dance in front of the bonfire was immediately summoned into the trance. She was suspended above the bonfire; her pupils constantly shuffling among the colors of the elements, gold, green, brown, sky blue, and silver.

"We are favored, we've found the new Soul Seeker," Illikus said, but the Men of the Counsel told him to be quiet.

"A seeker has never had a trance on her initiation," Izuk whispered softly to everybody present, "It doesn't portend something good. I wonder what she does see."

The woman made a sudden loud shrill that took everyone by surprise. She took her time as she spoke, "I see Jenagoa. I see the demon child. I see men with guns. Great trouble lies ahead."

ELEVEN

Bad people tell lies. Bad spirits tell even bigger lies. While Ben and Itherica's team foraged through the woods looking for the hidden twig, team Jenagoa never joined in the game. Luc, Tica, and Dale floated with Kyle high up in the air watching Itherica and Ben searching very eagerly.

"When are you going to tell them this is not a game Kyle?" Tica said to her mischievous counterpart. The glow in Kyle's eyes only meant more trouble. "They've been at it for almost an hour! You don't want them bumping into the others," Tica said with a bit of warning.

"Only a little while longer now," Kyle replied when he saw Ben and Itherica split up for only a short distance. "Itherica is not meant to find it."

Luc made an upset face. "So you never hid the twig in the first place; this isn't fun."

"I did," Kyle replied and smiled, "but Itherica is not going to find it. I hid it for her new friend to find."

Luc could fish out hostility in Kyle's attitude. "A ha a trick!" He smacked his lips in delight, "tell me Kyle."

Kyle didn't want to let the cat out of the bag yet, he called Dale. "You'll see, but first, let's separate them." Kyle and

Dale descended into the woods then disappeared. As they disappeared a thick fog slowly enveloped the trees.

"This is bound to be more fun than I thought," Luc said to Tica and beckoned, "Come let's go to see what Kyle's planned."

"Why?" Tica retorted and pouted. "Don't think I don't see between the lines here. Kyle is envious of that warm blood because Itherica loves him. Kyle is so foolish!"

"Kyle, envious?" Luc laughed, "Don't spoil our fun. All I see is—you are the one who's jealous. I know you've been jealous ever since Kyle returned Itherica's breath at the stream. You've been very jealous," he teased with a wry grin. "You'd always wanted her to die there, hadn't you? You wanted to take her breath and run away, huh?"

Luc pointed a crooked finger at Tica then laughed again. "Same here, but I'm different. I'm not striving for Kyle's attention."

"Oh shut up!" Tica said totally annoyed and disappeared.

"Pitiful sport," Luc laughed then disappeared to join the gang making the thick fog in the woods.

The fog came as a surprise. Itherica had only parted from Ben a stone's throw when the fog eased in, thick as smoke. She could barely see her hands. Ben was within hearing range but the more they yelled to each other, the farther away they seemed to separate. She could barely hear Ben when a hand shot up from the ground and grabbed her leg. It was cold.

"Wait!" a female voice said. It was Tica's and she was all around.

"Why do all of you like doing that?" Itherica exclaimed startled, and took a moment to catch her breath. She couldn't see Tica, the spirit was somewhere in the fog.

"You are so stupid, Itherica," Tica said with a bit of jealousy in her voice. "Why did you bring your friend here, did you think we'll all be jumpy and happy to see him?" she added very sarcastically.

"But you're my friends?" Itherica replied. "And he's my friend."

"You can't have two best friends, Itherica!" Tica snapped back. "You either love one more or love one less."

"That's not true," Itherica retorted. "We all can be best friends and play games..."

Tica interrupted very sternly, "When we found you, you were dead. And you'd still be dead by the stream if Kyle didn't spare your breath, Itherica. Everything was fine because we were the only friends you had. But now! Now you've done it! You've found a new pal and Kyle doesn't like you that way."

"That's not true, Kyle is always nice to me," Itherica replied and tried to find her way through the fog.

"Is that so?" Tica replied and said in a threatening tone, "I think you know very well what happens to warm bloods when they meet us?" Tica's voice seemed to fade away. "Remember, you were dead when we met you."

"You're scaring me Tica," Itherica replied, her voice quivering in newly found fear.

Tica remained silent.

"Ben!" Itherica screamed at the top of her voice, very nervously. There was no reply.

"It appears you've made your choice, Itherica." Tica said menacingly and disappeared.

"Ben!!"

The fog surrounding Ben seemed to thin out very quickly. He couldn't hear Itherica and was probably lost because everywhere in the woods looked the same, though there was somewhere bright shining at him from between the trees. So, Ben headed towards the light. There was an open space when he got closer. The open space was responsible for the bright light, since the daylight could reflect off the open surface of snow. He spotted a fairly large twig in the center of the snow in the open space and ran for it.

"Whoa," Ben said out loud once he stepped into the open space and almost slipped. It was slippery. He swept some snow off the surface with his boots and found ice underneath. He was standing on hard ice. "It's iced!"

"I see you've found it!" a voice said from a corner of the trees. The voice was Kyle's, and he was not alone.

The Jenagoa were waiting patiently for Ben to find the stream. Now the ill ploy was plain for Luc to see. It was the Scaba stream and everyone knew it flowed very viciously. But by this time of the year, the stream was frozen solid; on the surface that is, and Ben had no chance of knowing, a violent stream never stopped flowing. There were always one or two places where the ice was thin.

"You have to bring it to me to win!" Kyle yelled and waved an arm to Ben so the boy could see him.

"Hmm," Ben replied and carefully tottered to the large twig in the center of the iced stream. The ice was hard enough to walk across. He got to it. "Wow, it's larger than I thought," Ben whispered to himself, but it was a twin twig of the one Kyle showed him all right. The shape was exactly the same with the one Kyle had held in his arms. It was only bigger –a lot bigger.

"I don't think I can lift this?!" Ben yelled across the ice.

"Just drag it along the ice, dummy!" Luc yelled back, too excited to see Ben drown.

"Okay," Ben replied, rubbing his gloves together, "here goes." He tugged at the log and it slid along.

"Good. You're doing well," Kyle replied and Tica and Dale just watched from the sidelines. Their anxiety stole their concentration and the fog around Itherica began to thin out too quickly.

Ben tugged on it hard as it slid along. He lifted it a little and it slid even better, but then he heard Itherica's voice. The Jenagoa grew upset. Opposite the Stream, away from the Jenagoa, Itherica appeared, "Ben get off the Scaba. It's dangerous!"

"What!" Ben replied startled and dropped the twig immediately. The twig landed and the ice cracked in thin lines.

"Get off!!" Itherica gestured but it was too late. The rest of Ben's weight broke the ice and Ben fell underneath the ice into rough cryogenically running water.

The Phantom Publisher

Luc couldn't hide his glee, but Kyle only grew angrier when he saw the fear in Itherica's eyes. She jumped without second thought on the ice stream and ran to where Ben had fallen, kicking off as much ice as she could. Itherica could hear her heart beating.

TWELVE

Ice hunters told stories of drowning men. A drowning man only surfaced from the water three times. The water always let him. Any number less and he was already dead, but never a number more. That meant any rescue only had three chances to save a drowning man.

Ben's hand eventually broke through very thin ice many steps down the stream. The currents had him. "Ben!!" Itherica yelled and ran too fast to watch her step but stuck close to the bank of the stream. The ice was usually hard by the banks. She grabbed a twig, any twig hard enough to break ice.

Itherica felt a cold gust brush past her. "Don't try to save him," Kyle warned and appeared before her.

"Get away from me!" she retorted angry to the bones and slapped past his appearance. She looked downstream and upstream. Ben was nowhere to be found. Just then Ben's hand resurfaced through the ice a second time, but she had outshot his distance by a lot. She raced upstream then raced downstream, trying to determine how fast the current was carrying him. She feared her running was in vain because that was the second time Ben's hand reached through the surface.

"You won't save him by saving him," Kyle said wickedly, "let him go."

"I won't," Itherica yelled back and started hitting the ice with the stick, "I'm not like you!"

Kyle left misty hot in anger and reappeared along the banks, watching her hammering any spot that aroused her feelings.

"He's a dead boy," Luc said to Kyle at the stream bank. "I suppose his life breath will be escaping from the stream any moment now."

"I know," Kyle replied. He was still very angry and his mind was elsewhere.

"Let me have it, if you please?" Luc replied, thoroughly excited.

Itherica hit the stick hard on the iced stream and the twig snapped into two useless halves. She fell to her knees and a tear drop seemed to fall down her cheek for Ben. She had never laughed and cried on the same day.

Fortunately, Ben's hand broke through the ice right beside Itherica and his hand desperately grabbed for anything near. His hand grabbed the sleeve of Itherica's winter coat as he startled her. She was surprised. The Jenagoa were surprised.

"Ben!!" she screamed and laughed at the same time at the top of her voice and Itherica pulled on his arm so tightly. She never realized she was that strong. Itherica and Ben managed to break through the ice. He was very pale and cold stiff but his fingers were shivering. She wrapped him in her winter coat and took his off. She slowly pulled off everything warm she was wearing and put it on him. She wore his cold and wet clothes.

The Jenagoa slowly disappeared from the stream when Itherica found Ben. They were no longer on speaking terms with the demon child.

A Wolf was seldom alone. Gray wolves lived in closed societies and hunted in packs. Meals weren't easy to come by in the cold desert so every once in a while howls could be heard from across the ice. That alone made treading through the woods dangerous. The NASA boys were prepared for any good fight and were armed to the teeth. They were only half a day's walk to the Eskimo Village of Malagwa. But, more dangerous than hungry wolves with sharp teeth was the unseen danger of a vengeful and spiteful spirit lurking somewhere in the cold, planning mischief. It was easy for the Jenagoa to tell the NASA boys were friends with Ben since Captain Cain Cook occasionally yelled Ben's name at the top of his voice. With the exception of Elizabeth and Dr. Crawford, 5 NASA boys came along this time; Captain Cook, Nathan, Diego and the only engineer in the facility, Sergeant Benjamin. To the NASA boys they counted five men since Nathan was among them. The NASA boys had nicknamed Benjamin a Sergeant, because he was the only one among them who had served in the military.

They had reached the conifers that sheltered the Malagwan settlement from behind. The conifers were sparsely together but the thick bushes growing in between them made movement via motor sledges impossible, so the NASA boys abandoned their dogsleds outside the woods. From the woods on forth, they'd trek on foot to the Eskimo village.

"Ben!" Cain Cook yelled the nth time and Nathan placed a hand on his friend's shoulder.

"Don't worry, Mr. Cook, we'll find your boy," Nathan replied with a smile. Cain smiled back comfortably, but it was a brief and insincere smile.

"Look!" Nathan pointed to a black shadow racing across in the distance. "What do you think that is?" he asked, apprehensive.

"Wolves," Sergeant Benjamin replied calmly and cocked his rifle. "It's alright as long as you can see them," he added and sprung a quick pace in the lead of the group. "But don't take your eyes off them and don't expect them to be friendly," he warned, cautious of his every step, "Wolves are dangerous after dark."

Everyone double checked their arms and Diego navigated their way through the woods with the maps he held and the compass in his pocket. "That way," he pointed and they proceeded a bit further.

It didn't take long for a fog to develop. The fog snuck in subtly, but suddenly it was just there; thick for all to see, and getting much thicker by the minute.

"Well well, look at this?" Nathan said trying to see if he could see the yellow gloves he was wearing in the fog. He waved an arm in the air to everyone. "Can anyone see my arm at all?" he asked skeptically with a short laugh. "This mist is thick."

"It's a fog not a mist," Diego retorted since he knew better. He was a geologist. "A fog is thicker. Mists are thin," he answered to correct his colleague but the logic still didn't make him see any better. He tottered across the snow and slipped occasionally over some twigs buried in the snow.

"I've never seen anything like this," Captain Cook said with a strong sense of caution and everyone slowly became quieter. "Where did all this fog come from?"

"Probably the hills," Diego answered but his voice quaked uncontrollably. It was very obvious he was equally puzzled by the strange fog. And he still wasn't doing any better walking in the blinding fog. The fog was worsening. He really couldn't see his hands very well fully knowing he was wearing a black winter coat. "Sometimes air falls down steep slopes and carries with it whatever's suspended in it," he dared to continue his explanation, licking his lips. His mouth was dry.

"Whatever the reason, let's be cautious," Sergeant Benjamin warned firmly. "I don't like the way this fog feels. The last time I was in fog any bit similar to this, I was by a stream side in Vietnam," Benjamin clutched his gun much tighter, "– and it had bullets flying through it!".

"I agree," Captain Cook replied and he tried to stay alert in the fog.

When they could barely see their surroundings, the NASA boys heard a steady, strident growl but Cain Cook could almost swear he heard a child giggle.

THIRTEEN

Ben opened his eyes after a while. He was still cold and wasn't feeling so good to play, "I fell," he tittered to Itherica but she only stared down at him. He spoke but it wasn't Malagwan. "I don't think I want to play anymore."

Itherica was over Ben's face, grinning down at him. Her tears were almost blinding her. "Don't step on thin Ice," she warned sternly and put her warm hands on his face. Itherica was speaking clearly but it wasn't English. "Ben, can you get up?"

She gestured to lift him up.

"You want me to get up?" Ben said softly but she looked puzzled. Ben felt his clothes. They were Itherica's. "These are your clothes I'm wearing."

Itherica didn't understand him. He couldn't speak Malagwan anymore.

"I'll get it back," Itherica replied when she saw him touching the clothes, "but we have to go, it will be late soon."

"I can't understand you anymore Itherica," Ben said sadly, his lips still very pale, and sometimes he shivered in jolts. He touched her wet clothes, "but thank you."

"I'll give them back to you, if that is what you're asking?" She said, misunderstanding his gesture, but tried to help Ben to his feet. He was a little wobbly at the feet. "I'll prop you."

"Now I remember," Ben said and chortled, "We won, didn't we? We found the twig!"

Itherica hissed then looked around frightfully. All the mist had cleared. "We must go before they return. Quickly!"

"You mean the Jenagoa?"

Itherica pointed sealed lips to Ben and supported him through the woods.

Fire arms couldn't do squat if you couldn't aim at what you were shooting at. The NASA boys were at a disadvantage in the fog. They could hear the growls of the wolves but they could barely see themselves. On the other hand, the wolves had much more than just an excellent sense of smell; they were agile, fast, and armed to the teeth load. Everyone's fingers fiddled with their triggers in excitement but the excitement was too much for Cain Cook to handle, so he let some shots slip off the nozzle of his gun.

Everyone ducked their heads. "Watch how you handle that!" Sergeant Benjamin warned, pointing a finger at the captain.

The growls quieted for minutes, long enough for the NASA boys to believe all was well.

"You better watch where you point that thing, Cain," Nathan said to the captain from where he was standing. "You don't want to be picking what's left of me or anyone else from the ground. I can barely see you as we are."

"Don't badger him," Diego said out loud, relieved he could breathe now, "let's look on the bright side, he must have scared the wolves away,"

"I don't think you should handle a weapon," Sergeant Benjamin said to the air captain and searched through the fog for the captain's gun. "Let me have the gun."

"Don't take his gun from him," Nathan protested out loud, too loud and too carelessly in truth so everything happened in a flash.

A wolf jumped out of the fog for Nathan's face but the scientist dodged the animal by reflex. Yet the wolf's teeth caught him by the biceps. The wolf was heavy and pulled Nathan down to the snowy ground. It dragged him off almost immediately into the thick bushes. The NASA boys were stunned. It was either two or three wolves, but it was too foggy to tell.

"Nathan!" Captain Cook yelled and the NASA boys fired some gunshots in the direction Nathan disappeared into. A wolf whimpered but the fog enveloped all of Nathan. All that was left behind was the echo of Nathan's fainting shriek and lots of blood scattered about the place.

"Nathan!!" Cain Cook yelled again outraged. He wanted to run after the wolves in the fog but Sergeant Benjamin had a tight grip on him. "No. Stay back."

Nathan's screams deadened.

"Did anyone see their number? How many were they?" Sergeant Benjamin asked nervously, trying to whisper. His grip on Cain Cook was as tight as the grip on his voice.

"One. Three. Two." Diego said but he couldn't be precise. He was shaken to his nerves.

Some low growls could be heard and some slurping. Sergeant Benjamin fired a precise gunshot in the direction of the sounds. They heard another wolf whimper very loudly.

"Good shot, I think you got two of them," Diego said very nervously. His eyes wide open.

They all looked at each other and Sergeant Benjamin made up his mind to check out his kill. Cain Cook was near tears. Cain and Diego watched the sergeant slowly disappear into the fog.

A few yards behind some bushes, Sergeant Benjamin saw Nathan faint across the snow. Nathan's blood stained everything and everywhere.

Benjamin grew upset. "Nasty. What breed of wolves are these?" he mumbled to himself and found a dead wolf. It lay right beside Nathan with its blood on its teeth for Benjamin fortunately had shot a hole right through its head. He tried to touch it to see if it was dead, but at that moment another wolf leaped at him from nowhere. He managed to let off a shot, wounding the animal in one of its hind limbs, but he fell in the snow. And his gun fell even farther away. It was hard to see the butt of his gun sticking out of the snow in the fog so he reached randomly through the snow for it. The gun was already loaded so all that was left was for him to find it. The wounded wolf took its time to study the sergeant, growling in malice over the wound the sergeant had inflicted on its left limb. This wolf was big and his grey-white fur blending perfectly into the surrounding fog and snow. The moment Sergeant Benjamin felt the butt of his gun in the snow; the big wolf lunged for his jugular. He tried to pick up the gun in time but felt the gun pinned to the ground. He heard a child giggle and say, "Nah Nah, now don't cheat."

"What's going on here?" he exclaimed and looked up. He saw a child's face in the fog and it waved goodbye at him. By the time he remembered to look back, the wolf bit him hard; a lethal bite.

FOURTEEN

Hypothermia is an illness when a person's blood temperature reduces to a harmfully low degree and closely resembles death, but hypothermic fevers were more like malaria fevers. Although both are causes of people dying in way different parts of the world, fevers do break every once in a while, and during those fever breaks when one feels one's getting better that person's actually worse off.

The cold returned in his bones and Ben's shivers intensified. He had a severe headache but Ben couldn't tell Itherica since they spoke differently, or so he taught. A little closer to the Eskimo Village and Ben's knees collapsed. He couldn't support himself anymore. His sneezing had intensified and Itherica knew each sneeze would only make Ben weaker.

"But we are almost there?" Itherica asked a little frightful. She saw fatigue in Ben's face. He was going pale. "Okay, you need to rest then. Maybe we'll sit here a minute." She sat close to him and cuddled him close. It was an intelligent practice of the Eskimos to warm each other with collective body heat.

Itherica looked to the skies. The day was running late. Night was delayed by months in the cold desert but when it arrived, it arrived very quickly. The season of darkness was very deep and very dark.

"The Nachaga is coming," Itherica said looking to the darkening skies, darkening by the minute. "It's going to be dark very quickly," she said, sighing to rest by Ben's side.

"We don't see the Jenagoa at Nachaga," she said in a one way conversation. She didn't expect Ben to understand a word she was saying. "Kyle says they are not comfortable with the dark season, but do you want to know what I think?" Itherica asked with a chuckle. "I think they are plain scared of the dark!"

She smiled then cuddled Ben a little tighter when he sneezed again. Ben was breathing lightly.

"I don't like the Nachaga because it only brings me bad memories," she said, more to herself.

Ben managed to look up at her and she smiled at him. "It reminds me of my father, and two tricksters, Natrina and Etrica."

It didn't take long for Itherica to stumble into her side of the story, and what really happened in Malagwa 3 years ago; the day she lost her father.

3 years ago, at the onset of the Nachaga, Ithzermus led the Wolf Pack hunting and Malarina, Itherica's mother, went wood fetching with the women of Malagwa. The skies were much darker than they were now, so Malarina left Itherica in a friend's home with a playful vivacious girl, Etrica. In actual fact, it was Etrica with Itherica, since Itherica was the older of the two and she had to babysit Etrica. But Etrica wasn't alone that day, her cousin Natrina was down with the flu or so Natrina faked for all to believe. Natrina was much older

than Itherica and very sharp. And since she was sick, it was Itherica's job to watch over them both.

"Why don't we go play outside?" Natrina suggested with a harmless smile, still tucked in with a blanket over her legs.

"Yeah!" Etrica yelled and threw off her blanket. Itherica hesitated to get it. "Let's go outside!" Etrica repeated over and over and over again, jumping up and down her bed.

"What about your cold?" Itherica replied reluctantly, having plans to tell Etrica a story.

"Oh that," Natrina chuckled and hopped out of bed. "I faked that. Wood gathering is hectic and so boring," she yawned out her boredom. "Come on; now that we are free, let's do something fun. You don't want to remain cooked up in here do you?"

"Well?" Itherica was hesitant to think about it.

"Come on," Natrina went outside the Igloo, and the girls followed.

"I want to play snowman!" Etrica yelled over and over and over again.

Although it was growing darker, it was not dark enough to frighten the girls. The girls played themselves silly and though apprehensive at the onset, Itherica enjoyed every moment of it. That is every moment until Natrina suggested they play with the dogsled behind the Igloo. It belonged to Etrica's father and had a broken buckle, but the girls didn't know that.

"Daddy says we should stay away from the dogs," Etrica warned and Itherica took to the little girl's advice. "I don't want to get spanked," Etrica said in a gentle cry.

"What wrong with you both? Scared?" Natrina chided both girls. "You'll be riding one of these as soon as you're old enough."

"But she's not old enough," Itherica retorted. "Why don't we play with something else?"

"Don't worry about it," Natrina said and fed the hunting dogs. "They are much fun I promise, you'll get a real kick!" Natrina laughed and mounted the sled. She sped off and rode with such beauty. Natrina returned and picked Etrica on the sled. At first, Etrica was frightened to the bones, yelling and crying. Then she really enjoyed the ride.

"She didn't want to get off!" Itherica said to Ben. Ben couldn't take his eyes off Itherica. He could understand her clearly but he was too engrossed in her story to interrupt her. 'Go on', Ben's eyes seemed to say.

Itherica laughed when she remembered the delight on Erica's face, and had hopped on the sled without second thought.

"Slap it like this," Natrina showed her. "If you want to slow down, don't pull on the head dog first, okay?"

"Okay. I got all the instructions. Can I race it now?" Itherica asked Natrina impatiently.

"Let me on it! Please let me on it!" Etrica repeated over and over and over again, but Natrina held her back.

"Wait a minute, you'll get another turn," Natrina cautioned little Etrica and answered Itherica, "Race one circle, then we go on ours."

Itherica raced off but the speed with which she raced was overwhelming and worrisome. At first they were all laughing it out loud to ease their tension but then, unnoticeably, the broken buckle began to slip. The dogs were running too hard for the belt to hold any longer so the entire frame of the dogsled began to vibrate very violently.

Etrica pouted her lips while watching the dogsled lose control afar off, "I don't want to ride anymore, Natrina."

"Don't worry everything's going to be alright," Natrina replied to calm her little cousin. She watched Itherica hold on for dear life. Natrina bit her lips. "I hope so."

The broken buckle released a belt and the head dog ran off, probably back to the house. The dogsled was headless and raced wildly. It headed far off and too quickly into the woods with Itherica on it, still hanging on. The girls were scared, too scared to cry or panic.

Snow began to fall and the dogsled finally tired. All Itherica could hear were sounds familiar to the trickling of a stream. She walked for hours looking for it in the falling dusk and snow, probably in many circles. By the time she found it, she was weak and fainted after a drink from the Scaba stream.

Itherica sighed on seeing the sky darkening. She stood to help Ben up so they could head back to the Eskimo Village.

"So who rescued you?" Ben asked, and Itherica understood him clearly.

She gaped in awe and grabbed him in a hug. "You can hear me again? Good! But how come?" she rubbed her chin in a muse.

"I guess it comes and goes," Ben replied, "so who found you?"

"I don't know very well, but that was the first time I saw Kyle and Tica. They became my only friends after that."

"Huh, them? So that's why they call you Jenagoa," Ben replied and jolted, still having shivers.

"I see it now," Itherica said after musing and helped Ben to his feet, "I think I know now why you understand me sometimes and why at other times you don't."

"Why is that?" Ben asked.

"I think it always happens when they are nearby," Itherica replied and could swear there were mists in the forest around them. The falling darkness made it hard to tell. "You understood them, I mean my former friends, didn't you?"

"Yes, that's true," Ben answered. "That must be it."

"Let's get out of here. You don't look better." She hurried Ben and strangely his body temperature was beginning to sky rocket.

"What happened to Etrica and Natrina? Didn't they tell the truth?"

"No, they never did." Itherica replied very briefly.

"When we get back and I'm well enough I'm going to ask them why?" Ben retorted as Itherica propped him along.

"You can't Ben. Etrica and Natrina disappeared after the Nachaga that year."

"No one found them?" Ben asked in terror, but went quiet. "It wasn't you, I know. But now I know why everyone calls you demon child."

Itherica looked at Ben with a sad face. "They've been here all the while. Did you call them the name I told you not to call them since we've been talking?" she asked, a little frightened of the reply Ben might give.

"Yes," Ben frighteningly confessed then added, "but so did you, Itherica."

FIFTEEN

Cain Cook shot at the wolf square in the back and killed it, but he shot it twice to be on the safer side. Wolves were clever creatures, and crafty, and had a knack of surprising their enemy. The air captain found Sergeant Benjamin flat on his back gasping as blood oozed from his shoulder. The blood was a bright red color. Despite the severe bite wound the sergeant tried to talk. Cain Cook got on his knees to hold the Sergeant and keep him from talking; talking would only make the sergeant weaker. "Diego!" the air captain yelled for help.

Sergeant Benjamin made three fingers at Cain Cook. "Three? Three what?" the captain asked trying to understand what the Sergeant was trying to tell him. "Three wolves? There are three wolves?" he said and the Sergeant sighed, but it was already too late for Cain Cook to react; the last wolf lunged at Cain from behind. Cain Cook was lucky and spared Diego took a clear shot at it. The wolf scampered away bleeding profusely and running wildly into the woods. Oddly, the dense fog began to lift.

"He's hurt Diego," Cain Cook said sadly, "hurt badly."

The senses of the rock scientist were heightened by adrenaline and it took some minutes for Diego to calm his nerves and his senses to return to normal. Diego came over to take a look at the bleeding shoulder. "He'll live if I can get him to Crawford quickly enough."

Cain Cook heard some shuffling ahead and could make out Nathan's footwear in the lifting fog. He went over and found Nathan, eye's open and sprawled, in blood stained snow. But the blood was dark red in color. "He's alive, Diego!" Cain Cook yelled. "Nathan's alive. And he'll live! Nathan, can you hear me?"

"I must have passed out," Nathan replied, on seeing his friend stare down at him.

Cain Cook laughed, "You were dragged away by wolves. At least you're okay to talk. How are you feeling?"

"My whole body hurts," Nathan replied with a dry voice. "It seems I've been bitten everywhere except my face."

"Feel able to get up?" Cain asked but Diego yelled from behind, "Captain, we need to do something about the sergeant!"

"What happened to the Sergeant?" Nathan asked concernedly. The captain couldn't answer. "Cain? Tell me."

"Let me help you up," Cain said and helped Nathan to his feet. Nathan's body hurt a lot and streaks of blood oozed from the many bite wounds. He only stood with Cain supporting him.

Diego looked up at his friends as they approached from a distance. "Thank God you're alive. Seems like the wolves missed your vitals, though I can't say same for the sergeant; he is hurt bad." Diego looked to Cain for help. "The first aid kit is back with our dogsleds. I have to get the sergeant back to it now, but he'll still be in need of qualified medical attention. We're running out of options here, captain."

"You're right about that," Cain Cook said, his face looking desperate. "The fog is lifting too fast, and it's getting very dark all of a sudden."

"All isn't lost yet," Nathan said in between a lot of coughing. "All I need is to be bandaged up. I can still go with Cain to look for Ben. In the meantime, Diego can gain time returning the sergeant to Dr. Crawford."

Cain wasn't sure Nathan was strong enough and looked concerned, yet he couldn't voice his objection. Time was of the essence and it did sound like a good idea.

Nathan looked at Diego and instructed, "Use the radio on the sleds, Diego, so the good doctor can meet up with you halfway."

Since it was a good idea the men wasted no time getting to action. Nathan held Cain Cook by the shoulder as they prepared for what was to come. It was hard to lose friends.

Itherica and Ben reached Malagwa at the same time the Nachaga arrived over the Arctic in full visage. The darkness surrounding the village was intense and Ben was unconscious, taken by skyrocketing fever and violent shivers. But by the time Itherica reached Malarina's Igloo at the outskirts, Malarina was not the only person waiting for them. The Wolf Pack was waiting as well, along with the Counsel, and they forcefully parted Ben from Itherica.

"Let go of me!" Itherica struggled as they tried to calm her down, "He's sick. Why not leave us alone! Mother?!" she yelled.

Izuk appeared from nowhere. "Itherica," he said gently, "it's alright. We saw everything. We are here to help you."

Itherica calmed down and some lady dressed as the Soul Seeker approached her. The woman caressed Itherica's face tenderly, and she said, "so much in just one child, she's so brave and so beautiful."

There was a small bonfire some distance behind the Soul Seeker to give light in the Nachaga and it reflected in gold off Itherica's face. Itherica could see the fire clearly in the dark; that meant there was still time till the Jenagoa arrived Malagwa. But it was still 5 hours to midnight and the Nachaga wouldn't commence till then.

The plan was to keep the entire Malagwa gathered in one large tent. A huge bonfire was in the middle of the tent and the Soul Seeker performed healing rites over the young boy. She put fresh and bitter herbs between Ben's lips as she sang, chanted and danced. Malarina and Itherica sat quietly among everyone but there were still the occasional stares, not everyone trusted the demon child. Itherica didn't care; she was content having on warm clothes and watching Ben get better. There were herbs and potions everywhere. There were also guards posted around the tent and in formidable places around the little village. The guards were the company of the Wolf Pack.

Illikus called on Izuk for a private talk. Both men went outside the tent.

"What are you doing?" Illikus reprimanded the old man, "You know the Jenagoa are coming here for that child."

"Rest your concerns my child," Izuk replied, "by midnight the Nachaga will be complete. Till then we must protect everyone."

"Would you let your village perish?" Illikus said heatedly, there was a tone of bitterness in his voice.

"I am truly sorry for your loss," Izuk replied putting a hand on Illikus' shoulder. "I know what your boy meant to you, but don't take it out on an innocent girl. Save your energy."

Izuk headed back for the large tent.

"Well at least separate that woman and her child from the rest of the villagers! They'll put the others in jeopardy," Illikus said exasperatedly, and then said hesitantly, "I'll even offer them two of my best guards!"

Izuk nodded in response. "Alright, that would be appropriate." He walked back into the tent to let Itherica and Malarina know of the change in plans.

"I'm not going," Itherica said pouting her lips and locking her arms, "I want to watch my friend."

Just then two guards came in, waiting for the mother and child.

"But we have to," Malarina chided Itherica and got little Itherica on her feet. Illikus entered the tent. He had an evil look in his eye. "We have to," Malarina repeated frightfully.

"I'm not scared of him," Itherica tightened her lips and stood her grounds.

Izuk squatted and smiled at the little girl. "I promise no one will hurt you, Itherica. You only have to stay away till midnight."

"What about Ben? No one will hurt him?"

"No one will hurt Ben either," Izuk replied.

The Phantom Publisher

"Promise me," Itherica replied wittily.

"I promise," Izuk said raising an arm in oath. "I will watch over him till you and your mother return. Is that okay by you?"

Malarina and Itherica left the tent under the escort of two guards but no one at that time noticed that it had become a teeny bit cloudy to see the wood burning under the bonfire. It was now 2 hours before midnight.

SIXTEEN

The Malagwan believed the Balance of Fate was the balance between good and evil. It was a special balance that bound the spirit world and the flesh world to a mutual agreement of respect. Any way the balance topples carried a penalty. If good prevails, then evil was restrained by the same degree. And if evil prevails, then good was retrained likewise by an equal degree.

The Jenagoa had arrived. Kyle had arrived 2 hours before midnight, and Luc, Tica, and Dale weren't the only spirits that tagged along. They were all present; all and sundry. Immediately Malarina and Itherica got to their Igloo the two guards separated mother and daughter. One yanked Itherica away while the other trapped Malarina in the Igloo. Malarina screamed and Itherica struggled but it was all in vain. Illikus appeared from nowhere and Malarina knew they were betrayed.

"Guard the mother," Illikus commanded both guards and grabbed Itherica forcefully by the hands. "What no one dares to do, I will."

Itherica screamed at the top of her lungs and fought wildly. She scratched Illikus so hard, her fingers bled his arm. He grew upset and forgot she was a child. Illikus slapped Itherica hard across the face without thinking twice and she fainted. The guards were stunned.

"She brought it on herself! Jenagoa!" he muttered to himself and mounted unconscious Itherica on one of his broad shoulders. "I have to save what's left of Malagwa; I will offer her to them. You stay here." He commanded the guards, who were already having second thoughts.

He walked to a very conspicuous spot on the outskirts of the village. It was the usual market place everyone hung meats for sale. Still, it wasn't too far away to hear a gunshot.

Ben Cook was getting worse. The leaves weren't working and the skyrocketing fever was taking a toll on his body. He was beginning to exhale deeply and inhale very briefly. The soul seeker looked at his pale face and looked at Izuk. With one glance, Izuk knew the Jenagoa had arrived and the kid was breathing his last. The spirits were making him worse.

"We are going to lose this child," she said sadly, "the spirits are nullifying the healing process."

Izuk approached the Soul Seeker by the bonfire, "so the spirits are killing the child, how can we drive them away?"

The Soul Seeker looked directly at the bonfire and felt something strange, "The head of the Wolf Pack; Illikus. Find Illikus!" She demanded all of a sudden.

All the guards from the Wolf Pack spread out on hearing her orders.

"He escorts the child and her mother to their igloo. They will be safe there." Izuk replied the Soul Seeker but recognized that an old man at times could be naïve. "But what is the matter?" Izuk asked the Soul Seeker, his voice trembling to hear her reply.

The soul seeker's pupils turned gold looking at the bonfire, then sapphire blue, then grass green, and then returned to normal. She turned to Izuk and said, "Illikus has bitterness in his heart. You shouldn't have trusted him with the child. The only thing that prevents the Jenagoa from destroying the village is the balance of fate. If he kills the child, the Jenagoa will crush this village tonight."

She started her last dance when all in the tent heard a resounding gunshot. Everyone was startled and everyone rushed out. "Find Illikus!" Izuk screamed at the top of his lungs. Even the guards positioned to protect Ben in the tent rushed out. It was 40 minutes to midnight.

Illikus tied Itherica to a stake. He was going to leave her there alone for the spirits but Cain Cook and Nathan arrived in the nick of time. Both men noticed the man tying up a young child to a pole but Cain noticed something familiar when he came nearer. Cain Cook noticed Ben's winter coat! He pointed a rifle at the man tying up the child. "Put him down!" he commanded sternly. Nathan managed to cock his rifle and gesticulated to the young man to untie the child on the pole. Both men couldn't speak Malagwan, only Diego knew how to interact with the Eskimo folk.

"Please, put him down," Cain Cook said again, not lowering his gun though. "He's my son," the air captain tried to explain.

"No! Demon child! Don't touch!" Illikus yelled at the men in Malagwan, but they obviously didn't understand each other and a lot of tension was building up between them very quickly.

The Air Captain tried to lower his rifle not to scare the Eskimo man. He couldn't see Itherica's face in Ben's clothes since it was dark now and the impaled child was wearing the hood of the winter coat. Nathan kept his aim at the Eskimo man.

"What's wrong?! He's mine!" Cain Cook pointed to himself. He carefully approached the child and the Eskimo man violently shielded him from the child. "He's my boy! He's been missing for 2 days!" Cain begged loudly.

"Get away from the child," Nathan warned the Eskimo man, but in plain English. "Where's Diego to speak to this bum," Nathan said nervously pointing his rifle. "He looks dangerous to me."

"Demon child must remain here! Foreign child is in center square!" Illikus repeated violently over and over again, pointing to the center of the village from where the light of a huge fire was glowing. Cain and Nathan didn't understand a thing.

Illikus decided to remove the hood from Itherica but Nathan nervously let loose a gunshot. It ripped Illikus right shoulder and he groaned in pain. Cain Cook automatically untied the kid from the pole but when he pushed back the hood, he saw a beautiful girl child waking from a sour slap to the cheek.

"It's not Ben," Cain Cook said to Nathan, but shouldered the girl child. "He must be somewhere close by since she is wearing his clothes."

"Let's head to the center of the village," Nathan suggested, "I see some people rushing out of there."

Illikus groaned from his gunshot wound rolling in pain in the snow.

Cain Cook looked down at the groaning man, "should we help him?"

"No," Nathan replied with a vengeance, "Leave him there. Whatever the reason, no one should ever treat a child this savagely."

Izuk, the Soul Seeker, and the village were already on their way to the meat place. They met Cain Cook and Nathan along the way and both men were carrying the demon child. They promptly took Itherica from them and led them to where Ben was; the Wolf Pack needn't be told who both men were.

Illikus on the other hand was left wallowing in pain in the snow. Everyone nearby was outside earshot, they were all returning to the tent in the center of the village. A very cold gust brush past his face and he felt like the center of ominous gazes. The wind came from the top of the hills and when he looked to the hills, he saw them; dark silhouettes of little children staring down at him from the top of the hills. The moonlight illuminated their shapes clearly in the night light. The children were very many and he was frightened to his wits. He tried to get up and felt a very cold hand grab his leg.

"You wanted to hurt her didn't you!" a voice whispered from nowhere around him.

"No," Illikus lied and tried to scamper away.

Another cold hand grabbed his injured arm and he moaned out loud. "Don't lie to us, we saw you," another whisper bounced off his ears and he saw a young face build in the snow before him. He screamed for help as many misty arms pinned him down to the snow. Some of the spirits chuckled, giggled and laughed around him as they threw snow over him. They slowly started to make a snowman of him. He screamed one more time and Kyle shoved a handful of snow into his mouth, "Shush! Let's play a game."

SEVENTEEN

Everyone saw the spirits watching from the hills under the moonlight except the NASA boys. Cain Cook found his son by the bonfire, but by the time Nathan took a look at Ben, the boy was out of breath. He was cold stiff and pale. The life seemed to have breathed its way out of him. Cain Cook controlled his tears in quite sobs as he clutched the still body of his son in his arms. Itherica cried by Malarina and the whole tent was so quiet one could hear a pin drop. Nathan stood close by to console his friend. "It's my fault!" Cain Cook sobbed quietly. "I shouldn't have left him unwatched."

"It's their entire fault!" Itherica yelled in rage and Cain Cook turned to look at the young girl child. "They did this to him. They took him!" she shouted her hurt and in a rave tore out of her mother's comfort and ran outside the tent. It was a mystery that Cain Cook and Nathan could understand the child clearly. It was as though she spoke English. They followed the child outside, then Izuk and the Soul Seeker followed, and then all Malagwa. The Itherica child appeared delirious because she started screaming and yelling at the hills, but then Cain Cook and Nathan saw the little silhouettes standing on the top of the hills. The moonlight made the spirits visible.

Nathan was surprised. "What is that?" he couldn't refrain from asking. What he saw made him nervous. "They look like children."

"They are children," Cain Cook replied sternly while remembering the incident with the wolves and the giggle he heard in the woods hours before. He was still holding Ben in his arms, "A lot of children."

"You! Jenagoa!" Itherica yelled to the hills, totally out of control. "I hate you. I hate you all. You're wicked," she said over and over and over again, gathering handfuls of snow and throwing it in the direction of the spirits. "I hate you all a lot."

Malarina was the only woman who could calm her daughter but Itherica would not listen. Itherica could not be consoled. "Why not take me and leave this village alone! Why not take me and leave Ben all alone! Leave them all alone! Why won't you leave in peace? Take me and leave in peace!"

"Itherica!" Malarina ran for her daughter. "Please, you don't mean what you're saying!"

Itherica looked to her mother with very sad eyes, a lot of tears pouring down her eyes, "Yes, I do. Ben was my friend. I do mean it!"

The Soul Seeker approached Itherica to keep her from saying anymore but before she got to the child and her mother, Itherica slumped all of a sudden.

Everyone saw Itherica's skin going pale too quickly and too fast but Ben coughed instantly. Cain Cook was in shock. Ben began to warm up to normal body temperature quickly but Itherica was diminishing in strength and warmth.

"What's happening here?" Izuk asked the Soul Seeker, and the Soul Seeker had nothing but true tears in her eyes.

The Soul Seeker replied with a heartfelt cry, "Rite of Passage. She's making a trade with the Jenagoa. Itherica's trading her life for his."

Malarina sobbed softly as Itherica started to freeze over. Izuk put a hand on Malarina's shoulder and watched the boy get better. He said to Itherica, "He is okay."

Itherica smiled and slept before she went cold, as cold as death.

The Soul Seeker's said a second time, "so much in one child, so brave and so beautiful."

At that stroke of Midnight Itherica's eyes closed for the last time but Ben Cook opened his eyes.

"He's awake! He's awake!" Cain Cook exclaimed totally delighted and hugged his little boy but when Cain looked up, all Malagwa was in mourning. It was a life for a life.

That Night the Balance of Fate tipped in the side of the Malagwan and the Jenagoa faded away from the hills into the Nachaga without a single objection.

Much later, when Ben Cook was strong enough to talk, he asked Cain Cook and any who could answer him, "Where's Itherica? Where's my friend?"

EIGHTEEN

The NASA boys arrived home prematurely in Richmond, Canada. Ben Cook didn't say a word even when Captain Cook landed the plane and drove for home.

"Your mother will be glad we are home safe, lad?" Captain Cook said to the young lad when he opened the door to their home.

"Who is it?" Ben's mother yelled from the kitchen. Catherine Cook came out in aprons but Ben walked in silently and quickly ran upstairs for his bedroom.

Catherine Cook watched her son storm up the stairs and Ben slammed the door to his room. She looked to her husband. "What's that all about?"

Cain Cook took off his pilot's cap and hugged his wife tenderly. "A lot has happened, my dear. You are about to hear a long story."

Ben's room was very simple. There was a bed, a television, a computer, a book shelf, and Ben's study table. Catherine Cook had placed a full glass of water on the study table alongside a water jug. Ben locked the door to his room door and fell on his comfy bed. It wasn't so comfy anymore. He was sad. It was hard to lose friends. But the moment Ben was about to fall asleep his warm bedroom went cold, very cold. Ben sat up and looked around. The full glass of water

The Phantom Publisher

was almost empty. Something or someone misty was flying around in the room.

"Jenagoa?" he muttered, wanting to run out of his room.

"Don't call me that silly!" Itherica answered and formed in a cloud on Ben's bed. "I am not like those rascals. They are asleep now."

"Wow. How can you be alive? But you died," Ben stuttered not believing his eyes.

Itherica pounced about Ben's room looking amused then replied wittily, "Not even death can separate close friends, remember that!"

Ben couldn't hide his smile. "You like my room?"

"Yes, I do," Itherica said smiling. "It's very nice."